Saving STRAWBERRY FARM

BY DEBORAH HOPKINSON

PICTURES BY RACHEL ISADORA

GREENWILLOW BOOKS

An Imprint of HarperCollinsPublishers

Library of Congress Cataloging-in-Publication Data
Hopkinson, Deborah.
Saving Strawberry Farm / by Deborah Hopkinson;
pictures by Rachel Isadora.
p. cm.
"Greenwillow Books."

Summary: During the Great Depression, Davey learns that a neighbor's property
is about to be auctioned, and he rallies his friends, neighbors, and family to help
save Strawberry Farm.

ISBN 0-688-17400-0 (trade). ISBN 0-688-17401-9 (lib. bdg.)
1. Depressions—1929—Juvenile fiction. [1. Depressions—1929—Fiction.
2. Neighborliness—Fiction. 3. Auctions—Fiction. 4. Country life—Fiction.
5. Fourth of July—Fiction.]
I. Isadora, Rachel, ill. II. Title.
PZ7.H778125Sav 2004 [E]—dc22 2003012565

First Edition 10 9 8 7 6 5 4 3 2 1

 GREENWILLOW BOOKS

FOR MICHELE, SHERIDAN, AND KRISTIN
—D. H.

FOR LIBBY SHUB
—R. J.

THE SUN WAS SO MEAN THAT SUMMER,
it seemed to chase all the clouds away.

"It's hot enough to fry an egg on the street," Dad said.

I wondered if an egg really would fry. But we couldn't waste one to try it. Mom made us eat just about every egg our scrawny chickens laid.

That summer, there wasn't much else.

Before, when Dad worked regularly, our icebox was full of food. To keep it cold, we put a card in the window to tell the iceman how much ice to deliver. And every day after school, Mom fixed us cold, sweet lemonade in tall glasses, with big chips of sparkling ice.

But that was before.

Before Dad and just about everyone else lost their jobs. Before times got hard.

Now we only kept one room lit after dark. We made do with our old clothes. We didn't eat meat.

The iceman didn't come to our house anymore, either.

"TOMORROW'S THE FOURTH OF JULY," Dad said. "No matter how bad things are, it's still our country's birthday. Maybe we could have a picnic, like we used to."

Mom brightened. "Well, I suppose we could buy a block of ice and make lemonade. I might have enough sugar saved back for cookies."

Mom gave me a dime from the tin. "Get a block of ice from Mr. Russell's store, Davey. Take Dad's old yellow raincoat to wrap it in. You and little Rose come right back. Don't let it melt."

After the bright sun, the inside of Mr. Russell's store seemed dark. But Rosie knew just where to go.

She streaked past canned goods and bolts of cloth, hammers, nails, and chicken feed, and barrels of flour and cornmeal.

Straight to the candy counter.

Somehow candy always looked better when we didn't have money—red hots and peppermint sticks, lemon drops and malted milk balls, long strings of licorice.

Mr. Russell spotted me. "Davey, help Miss Elsie out with her grocery bag, will you? I got to fetch some sugar from the back for Mrs. Stone."

Everyone knew Elsie Elkins. She had the prettiest strawberry farm in the county. Mom took us strawberry picking every June. We'd come home with flats of plump, juicy fruit—enough to make jam for the whole winter.

Miss Elsie never minded if you ate while you picked. I liked to find the fattest, reddest strawberries hiding deep under the leaves. When you put one in your mouth, it was like tasting summer.

I followed Miss Elsie out to her Ford Model A truck. "Can I work for you next year, Miss Elsie? I'll be old enough."

"Davey, there probably won't be a Strawberry Farm next summer. . . ." She sighed.

Miss Elsie pulled out an old brown penny from her purse. "I don't have many pennies left, but I still like to tip a good boy."

I held the penny tight as the truck chugged away.

Rosie's eyes got round when she saw the penny. Would I choose caramels or red hots? Suckers or Tootsie Rolls?

Then I heard Mr. Russell's voice, gray as a thundercloud. "Shame about Elsie losing Strawberry Farm."

"When's the auction?" Mrs. Stone asked.

"Tonight. Five o'clock."

So that's what Miss Elsie meant. "Why is she losing the farm?" I wanted to know.

"Can't keep up her payments to the bank," Mr. Russell told me, wrapping up a poke of sugar for Mrs. Stone.

"That's not fair," I cried. "Lots of people don't have much money now."

Mr. Russell leaned on the counter. "Boy's got a point," he said in a low voice. "Maybe we should try a penny auction."

"What's that?" I asked.

"Usually the person who offers the most money at an auction gets the farm," explained Mr. Russell. "But at a penny auction, everyone gets together to keep the bids real low. That way Miss Elsie can afford to buy her own farm back."

"The bank folks don't like penny auctions," Mrs. Stone added. "So the whole town has to get behind it. How can we let folks know in time?"

"Davey, I bet Miss Elsie gave you that penny you're holding on to so tight," said Mr. Russell. "Now, on your way home, you show that to everyone you see. Tell them to come to the auction."

"Don't forget to show the penny," Mrs. Stone added. "Folks will know what it means."

ROSIE DROPPED HER END OF THE HEAVY block of ice.

"Why couldn't we buy candy?" she whined again.

"I told you. This penny is special, like a secret code. Come on, Rosie," I growled. "We have to hurry."

If only I had a wagon.

If I had a wagon, I could fetch ice by myself. Without a tagalong little sister.

Once I cut out a picture of a shiny red wagon in the Sears catalog and kept it in a box under my bed. But after a while, I stopped hoping for it and tore it up.

We walked down Maple and up Holly Street. Most people, like Dad, didn't have jobs. So folks were sitting on front porches or working outside.

Mrs. Moore was in her garden, the best in town. Sometimes Mom would give me half a dozen eggs to trade for lettuce, peas, or carrots.

"If anyone deserves help, it's Elsie Elkins," she said, wiping the sweat from her forehead. "That lady's as sweet as the strawberries she grows."

NEXT WE TOLD DAD'S FRIEND TED.
Since he'd lost his job at the factory, he spent most days
carving spoons from wood. Ted was always trying to sell them
for a few pennies or trade them for food.

"I'll be there," he said. "Make sure you tell Nellie Hall. She's
got a telephone and can pass the word."

We went up and down the streets, showing the penny.

"Wherever have you been? That ice must be melted!" Mom
cried when we finally got home.

Dad's raincoat was a little drippy, I noticed.

I held up the penny once more.

"We have to help save Strawberry Farm!"

BY FIVE O'CLOCK MISS ELSIE'S DUSTY YARD was full of people talking quietly and fanning themselves in the heat. I climbed up on the back of Miss Elsie's truck to see over all the heads.

Mrs. Stone smiled at me. "You did a good job, Davey. Look at this crowd!"

A skinny man in a gray suit stood on a wagon, waving his hand in the air.

"Now, folks, we're here to auction off this nice farm," the man said. "Serious bids only, please."

The crowd grew silent, as though the shadow of a hawk had passed overhead.

The man cleared his throat. "How about someone starting off with a bid of three hundred dollars?"

Around me the grown-ups gasped. Three hundred dollars! That was too much. If someone made a bid that high, Miss Elsie could never buy her farm back.

Folks stared at the ground, shuffling their feet in the dry dust. The silence deepened.

Nobody wanted to be the first to speak up. Maybe, I thought, everyone's afraid of the bank man.

"Come on, folks . . ." said the auction man.

I felt nervous. I stuck my hands in my pockets. Miss Elsie's penny was still there. I could see her standing near the front, her shoulders straight and thin under her summer dress.

I took a deep breath, held up the penny, and yelled as loud as I could.

"One penny for Strawberry Farm!"

Every head turned toward me. The auction man's face flushed red as an overripe berry.

He opened his mouth to yell.

But before he could, Mr. Russell slapped his thigh and shouted, "I'll raise Davey's bid to a dime, mister!"

"Two bits," yelled Dad.

Ted waved one of his spoons in the air. "One dollar even."

Suddenly the crowd came alive with bids, each higher than the next—but only by a nickel, a dime, or two bits.

And if anyone still thought of offering a lot of money, well, he or she wouldn't do it now. Our town wouldn't stand for it.

When the bidding got up to nine dollars and fifty cents, Miss Elsie's voice rang out.

"Nine dollars and seventy-five cents for Strawberry Farm!"

And that was it. The last bid.

There was nothing the auction man could do except sell the farm back to Miss Elsie.

People passed a hat and threw in coins to help Miss Elsie come up with the money.

Afterward she walked through the crowd, smiling, and climbed up beside me on her little truck.

"Thank you, dear friends, for this wonderful gift," she said, her voice shaky with tears. "And if I can make it till spring, you're all invited to come pick some strawberries for free!"

I watched the sun sink low until it touched the fields and made their poor dryness glow like a hopeful new penny.

The cool night air felt so good no one wanted to leave Strawberry Farm. Or maybe we knew we'd made something special together, something we didn't want to break apart.

On the way home, Dad carried Rosie on his shoulders. Mom and I counted fireflies.

"Almost as good as firecrackers," she whispered.

We didn't have a picnic for Independence Day after all. Mom and Dad had given all their extra coins to help buy Strawberry Farm.

We still had some ice, though.

And we sat on the stoop talking to our neighbors, drinking cold lemonade full of big chips of sparkling ice that bounced against our noses.

I PUT MISS ELSIE'S PENNY IN THE BOX
under my bed. I figured I had to start somewhere to save for a
wagon. And maybe, next summer, I'd get to work on
Strawberry Farm.

There were lots of times I almost spent that penny on candy.
But I never did.

AUTHOR'S NOTE 🖋

This story takes place during the Great Depression, which began in October 1929 and lasted for almost ten years. The Depression affected millions of children like Davey and Rose and their families. More than 12 million people lost their jobs when factories, stores, mines, and even banks closed. All over the country, people struggled to survive with little work, money, or food.

To make matters worse, the 1930s were years of terrible drought, heat waves, and fierce dust storms. Many farmers lost their farms when food prices dropped and crops failed, and they could no longer make their mortgage payments to the bank.

Many people thought this was unfair in such hard times. Sometimes, when the bank was about to take a farm back (called a foreclosure) and sell it at an auction to someone else, the community stepped in to help. Just as in this story, friends and neighbors would come together and bid so low that the original owners could buy back their own farm. Eventually, some states passed laws that stopped foreclosures until times were better for farmers.

In 1932, Franklin Delano Roosevelt was elected president. He created programs to help people and give them jobs. These programs became known as the New Deal. The New Deal did much to help families recover from the worst economic crisis in our country's history.

MR. RUSSELL'S STORE 🖋

Have you ever been to a neighborhood store like the one Davey and Rose visited? In the 1930s there were many more small "Mom and Pop" stores than there are today. Most have been replaced by large supermarket chains. Here are some of the items you might have found in Mr. Russell's store. What else do you think a neighborhood store might sell?

Big bulk containers of rice, flour, dried peas, and beans	Kegs of pickles
Lard in metal cans	Cracked or shelled corn for chickens
Dry goods, such as bolts of calico and muslin	Needles, pins, and handkerchiefs
Work gloves and tools	Dried apricots and raisins
Baskets of fresh fruit in summer and fall	Penny candy

ACKNOWLEDGMENT 🖋

Research for this story was greatly aided by two memoirs of the Depression written by Robert J. Hastings entitled *A Nickel's Worth of Skim Milk* (1972) and *A Penny's Worth of Minced Ham* (1986), both published by Southern Illinois University Press. Mr. Hastings tells many stories about his boyhood and the neighborhood stores in Marion, Illinois. According to Mr. Hastings, a "poke of sugar" was a pound of sugar in a paper sack.